The Discovery of Longitude

The Discovery of Longitude

By Joan
Marie
Galat

Illustrated by
Wes Lowe

PELICAN PUBLISHING COMPANY
Gretna 2012

For Arden, with love—JMG

The word "Pelican" and the depiction of a pelican are
trademarks of Pelican Publishing Company, Inc., and are
registered in the U.S. Patent and Trademark Office.

Library of Congress Cataloging-in-Publication Data

Galat, Joan Marie, 1963-
  The discovery of longitude / by Joan Marie Galat ; illustrated by Wes
Lowe.
    p. cm.
  ISBN 978-1-4556-1637-4 (hardcover : alk. paper)—ISBN 978-1-4556-
1638-1 (e-book) 1. Longitude—Measurement—History. 2. Chronometers-
-History. 3. Harrison, John, 1693-1776. 4. Clock and watch makers—
Great Britain—Biography. I. Title.
  QB225.G36 2012
  526'.62—dc23
                                        2011052911

Printed in Singapore
Published by Pelican Publishing Company, Inc.
1000 Burmaster Street, Gretna, Louisiana 70053

The Discovery of Longitude

More than 300 years ago, explorers traveled the seas in great sailing ships. They often got lost. Maps were not very good and stormy weather could blow ships out to sea or hurl them into rocks. Wind could rip their sails or steer them in the wrong direction. Lost sailors died if they ran out of food and fresh water.

Sailors found their way more easily when they could see land. Captains tried to sail close to shore, looking for landmarks like mountains and rivers. They had to guess which way to go when they couldn't see land.

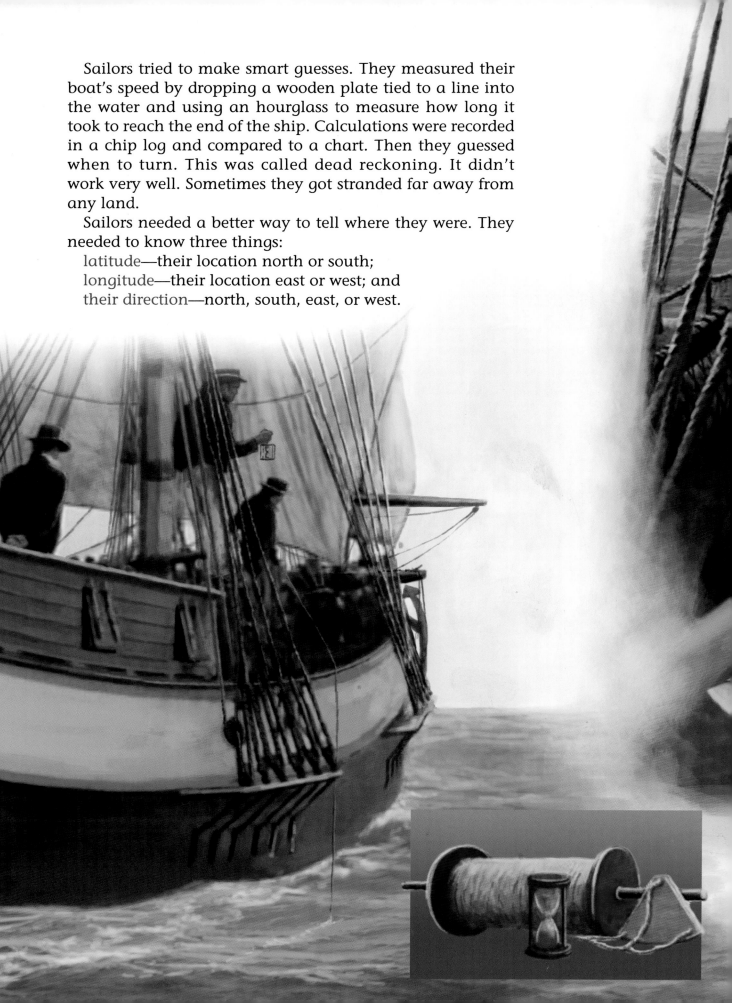

Sailors tried to make smart guesses. They measured their boat's speed by dropping a wooden plate tied to a line into the water and using an hourglass to measure how long it took to reach the end of the ship. Calculations were recorded in a chip log and compared to a chart. Then they guessed when to turn. This was called dead reckoning. It didn't work very well. Sometimes they got stranded far away from any land.

Sailors needed a better way to tell where they were. They needed to know three things:

latitude—their location north or south;
longitude—their location east or west; and
their direction—north, south, east, or west.

Captains used a compass to find direction. The needle in a compass always shows north. But there were still problems with this method. Salt water made compasses rusty. Compass needles also jiggled when ships rocked on ocean waves. The needle jiggled too much to read.

It was easier to figure out the ship's location when skies were clear. At night, sailors found north by looking for the North Star. During the day, they looked for the Sun, because it rises in the east and sets in the west.

Sailors knew how to figure out latitude. They used a tool called a sextant to find their position north or south of the equator. Sextants measure the height of the Sun and stars above the land.

The captain compared numbers from the sextant to latitude lines and numbers on a map. This showed how far north or south the ship was from the Earth's equator—the imaginary line that divides the Earth's top and bottom halves.

Sailors still needed a way to figure out longitude—their position east or west. They could measure distance if they knew the exact time. It sounds tricky until you think about how time is measured.

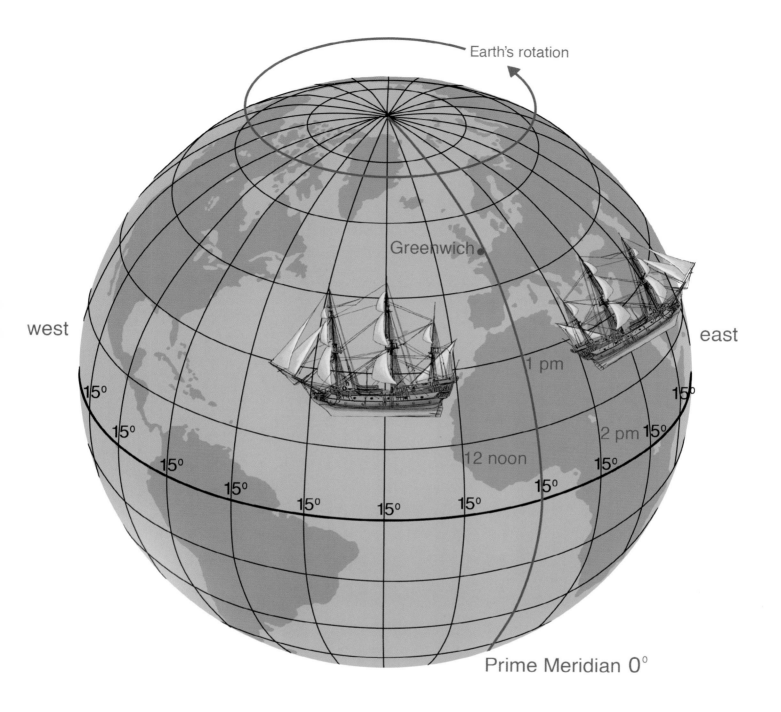

The Earth turns 15 degrees every hour. This makes a twenty-four-hour day. When someone travels 15 degrees east, time moves ahead one hour. When someone travels 15 degrees west, time moves back one hour.

Meridian lines on maps show each one-hour time change. Every line is 15 degrees apart. One of the lines is at Greenwich, England. English sailors used this line to mark zero degrees longitude. They called it the prime meridian.

The prime meridian is an imaginary line. It divides the Earth's east and west halves. Sailors could use the prime meridian to figure out how far they needed to travel east or west, if they knew the correct time.

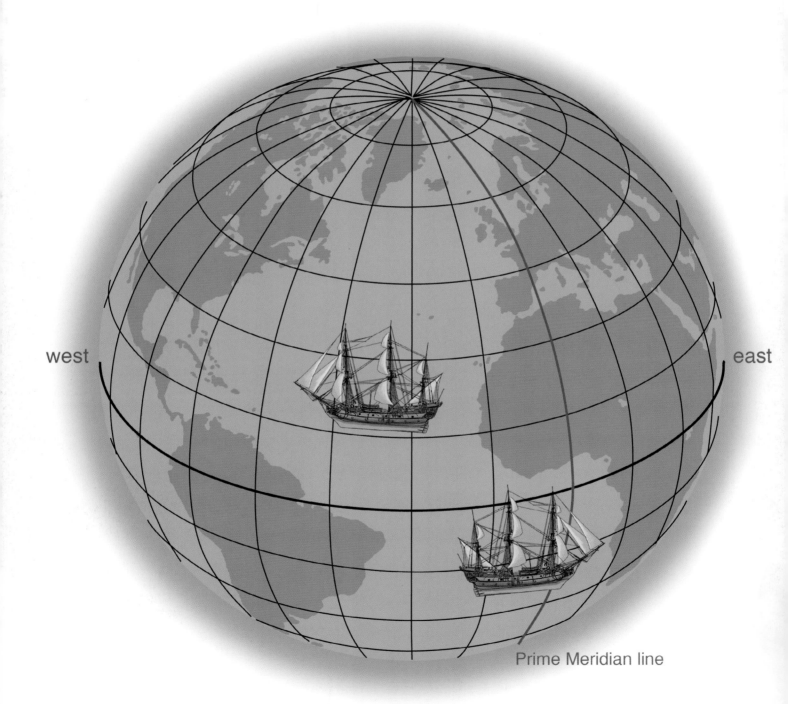

west

east

Prime Meridian line

They needed two numbers—the time on the ship and the time in Greenwich. There was still one problem! Clocks in the 1700s were not very exact.

Pendulum clocks, which use a swinging weight to measure time, did not work well on moving ships. Temperature changes, moisture in the air, and the motion of the ship made clocks run poorly. Watches were no better. Salt water made them rust. No one knew what to do!

Sailors could get lost if their clock was wrong by even a few seconds. In 1707, twenty-one British ships sailed into fog. They did not know where they were. All the ships crashed into rocks. Two thousand men died.

The British government wanted to stop navigation accidents from happening. In 1714, they offered £20,000 to anyone who could figure out longitude. This would equal more than three million US dollars today! Many people thought it was an impossible problem to solve. They said only fools and lunatics would try!

John Harrison was a carpenter who built clocks. He tried to make a clock that worked in a rocking boat. One of his clocks kept time using springs instead of a pendulum. It weighed seventy-two pounds!

His clock worked well, but not well enough. The carpenter kept trying. He made two more clocks. Each clock worked better than the last, but none worked well enough to solve the problem and win the big prize.

Harrison decided to start all over. He designed a pocket watch for his own use. The watch kept very good time! Harrison thought he could make it work well enough to use at sea.

He built a clock that looked like a large pocket watch. It was 5.1 inches in diameter and weighed 3.2 pounds. Harrison's son, William, tested the watch on a ship called the HMS *Deptford*. It left for Jamaica on November 18, 1761.

The HMS *Deptford* reached Jamaica about a month later. Harrison's clock was only 5.1 seconds slow! He worked on it for two more years. His next clock was tested on a ship sailing to Barbados in 1764.

William sailed to Barbados too. His job was to make sure the watch was wound each day. Harrison's new watch kept the best time. It was good enough to win the prize!

The Board of Longitude did not want to give Harrison the money. They said they needed more proof that his invention worked. The board offered Harrison half the prize in exchange for his clocks, watches, and designs.

At first, he refused. But after several weeks, Harrison and his son gave the board what they wanted. William was upset and wrote a letter to King George III. The king was interested in science. He tested the timepiece himself and became angry that Harrison was not given the full prize. He complained to the Prime Minister, who ordered Harrison be paid.

In 1773, Harrison received the prize money. Now eighty years old, he had worked on the longitude problem for forty-three years. His inventions made sailing much safer. Many countries used his clocks. Several countries also used Greenwich as the prime meridian.

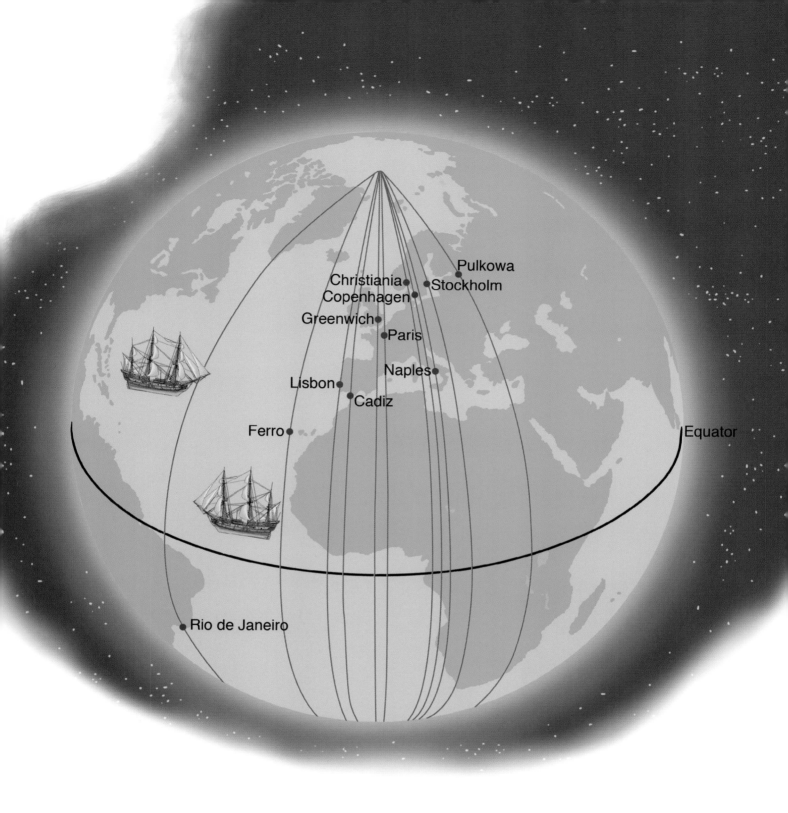

Some countries used other meridian lines for zero longitude. This made travel confusing. One hundred years after Harrison solved the longitude problem, the United States government organized a meeting to decide which longitude line should be the official prime meridian.

People from twenty-five different countries met in Washington, DC. They named Greenwich the Prime Meridian of the world. Now all countries figure out time the same way. Navigation is easier and safer with everyone using identical time, longitude, and latitude.

Harrison's Work on the Longitude Problem

1737 . . . . John Harrison presented the Board of Longitude with his first marine timekeeper, Harrison-1, called H-1.

1741 . . . . Harrison presented H-2 but still thought he could improve it.

1758 . . . . Harrison created H-3. It was never tested at sea, first because of the Seven Years War (nobody wanted to risk losing it in an ocean battle), and then because Harrison made H-4. (Eighteen years later.)

1760 . . . . . . John Harrison completed H-4, which he called "the watch." It was smaller and easier to handle than H-1 to H-3.

1761-62 . . . . The watch was tested on a transatlantic voyage. It was precise enough to claim the £20,000.

The Board of Longitude was reluctant to pay the prize and asked Harrison to explain the mechanism. He refused. The board decided a second trial voyage should be made, and in 1764 William sailed to the West Indies with H-4. It performed three times better than required by the Longitude Act.

The Board offered Harrison £10,000 for all four timekeepers and his plans for H-4. They wanted him to build two duplicates of H-4 before awarding the rest of the prize.

1770 . . . . Harrison finished the first copy, called H-5. He was getting older. It was doubted that he could make another watch.

1772 . . . . Harrison's son, William, wrote to King George III and described his father's hardship. The King ordered that Harrison be awarded another £8,750.

1773 . . . . The Longitude Board awarded Harrison and his son £8,750.